THE DOOMED TOWER

Ethan Flask and Professor von Offel's
Adventures in Engineering

MAD SCIENCE

by Kathy Burkett

SCHOLASTIC INC.

New York   Toronto   London   Auckland   Sydney
Mexico City   New Delhi   Hong Kong

Table of Contents

Prologue

For more than 100 years, the Flasks, the town of Arcana's first family of science, have been methodically, precisely, safely, *scientifically* inventing all kinds of things.

For more than 100 years, the von Offels, Arcana's first family of sneaks, have been stealing those inventions.

Where the Flasks are brilliant, rational, and reliable, the von Offels are brilliant, reckless, and ruthless. The nearly fabulous Flasks could have earned themselves a major chapter in the history of science — but at every key moment, there always seemed to be a von Offel on the scene to "borrow" a science notebook, beat a Flask to the punch on a patent, or booby-trap an important experiment. Just take a look at the Flask family tree and then at the von Offel clan's. Coincidence? Or *evidence*!

Despite being tricked out of fame and fortune by the awful von Offels, the Flasks doggedly continued their scientific inquiries. The last of the family line,

Ethan Flask, is no exception. An outstanding sixth-grade science teacher, he's also conducting studies into animal intelligence and is competing for the Third Millennium Foundation's prestigious Vanguard Teacher Award. Unfortunately, the person who's evaluating Ethan for the award is none other than Professor John von Offel, a.k.a. the original mad scientist, Johannes von Offel.

Von Offel needs a Flask to help him regain the body he lost in an explosive experiment many decades ago. In the meantime, von Offel is creating all sorts of havoc. In *Foul Play! Ethan Flask and Professor von Offel's Sports Science Match*, the professor went so far out of bounds that he almost sidelined the Einstein Elementary School's soccer team, too!

Professor von Offel is also getting very careless about hiding his real identity. Prescott, Luis, and Alberta know he's a ghost, but they realize they must keep von Offel's secret or risk scuttling Mr. Flask's chances of winning the Vanguard Teacher Award. They even have to protect the professor's identity from their suspicious classmate, Max Hoof. And now that von Offel has abandoned all efforts at disguising himself, he can really concentrate on rebuilding himself — *all* of himself, that is!

You'll find instructions for the experiments similar to the ones mentioned on pages 6, 9, and 33 of this book in *Engineering Science*, the Mad Science Experiments Log.

The Nearly Fabulous Flasks

Jedidiah Flask
2nd person to create rubber band

Oliver Flask
Missed appointment to patent new glue because he was mysteriously epoxied to his chair

Augustus Flask
Developed telephone; got a busy signal

Mildred Flask Tachyon
Tranquilizer formula never registered; carriage horses fell asleep en route to patent office

Lane Tachyon
Developed laughing gas; was kept in hysterics while a burglar stole the formula

Percy Flask
Lost notes on cure for common cold in pick-pocketing incident

Archibald Flask
Knocked out cold en route to patent superior baseball bat

Marlow Flask
Runner-up to Adolphus von Offel for Sir Isaac Newton Science Prize

Amaryllis Flask Lepton
Discovered new kind of amoeba; never published findings due to dysentery

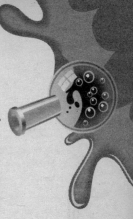

Norton Flask
Clubbed with an overcooked meat loaf and robbed of prototype microwave oven

Salome Flask Rhombus
Discovered cloud-salting with dry ice; never made it to patent office due to freak downpour

Roland Flask
His new high-speed engine was believed to have powered the getaway car that stole his prototype

Constance Rhombus Ampère
Lost Marie Curie award to Beatrice O'Door; voted Miss Congeniality

Margaret Flask Geiger
Name was mysteriously deleted from registration papers for her undetectable correction fluid

Michael Flask
Arrived with gas grill schematic only to find tailgate party outside patent office

Solomon Ampère
Bionic horse placed in Kentucky Derby after von Offel entry

Ethan Flask

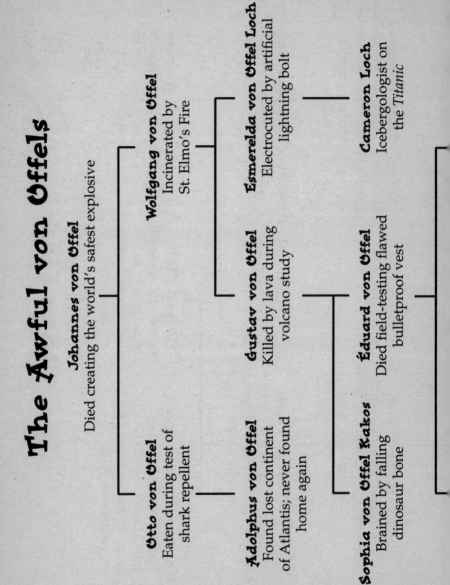

The Awful von Offels

Johannes von Offel
Died creating the world's safest explosive

Otto von Offel
Eaten during test of shark repellent

Wolfgang von Offel
Incinerated by St. Elmo's Fire

Adolphus von Offel
Found lost continent of Atlantis; never found home again

Gustav von Offel
Killed by lava during volcano study

Esmerelda von Offel Loch
Electrocuted by artificial lightning bolt

Sophia von Offel Kakos
Brained by falling dinosaur bone

Eduard von Offel
Died field-testing flawed bulletproof vest

Cameron Loch
Icebergologist on the *Titanic*

Rula von Offel Malle
Evaporated

Beatrice Malle O'Door
Drowned pursuing the
Loch Ness Monster

Feldspar O'Door
Died of freezer burn
during cryogenics
experiment

Kurt von Offel
Weak batteries in
antigravity backpack

Colin von Offel
Transplanted his brain
into wildebeest

Alan von Offel
Failed to survive field
test of nonpoisonous
arsenic

Felicity von Offel Day
Brained by diving bell
during deep-sea
exploration

Professor John von Offel (?)

Johannes von Offel's
Book of Scientific Observations, 1891

Jedidiah Flask has once again shown himself to be a man of small dreams. His latest idea is to take tons of steel and fashion it into an ordinary tower. His lowly aim? To give his volunteer fire brigade a perch from which to scan the surrounding forests for smoke and flames. Certainly that feeble band of do-gooders has its place. They've even helped extinguish the odd fire around my house on a handful of occasions this year. But why should their structure be the tallest in Arcana? Naturally, I've taken Flask's stunted tower as a dare. I will start with the same tonnage of steel and a building site very near his. But what will rise from that site will be pure von Offel genius. I've calculated that by cutting out all of the fussy cross bracing, I can go nearly 50 percent higher. When Flask saw my brilliant design, he cried foul. He claimed to have safety in mind and threatened that the town building inspector would never approve my plans. That just goes to show how poor his grasp of civic matters is. Blackmail is a proud von Offel tradition and has smoothed the way for more than one of my family's construction projects.

CHAPTER 1

A Tale of Two Towers

D r. Kepler burst into the sixth-grade science lab waving a gold-edged piece of paper. "Congratulations, Ethan! You got the grant!" The principal crossed to the front of the room and gave Mr. Flask a high five.

Lab assistants Alberta Wong, Luis Antilla, and Prescott Forrester were just settling into their seats. They looked at one another, eyebrows raised, then glanced back at Professor von Offel's empty desk.

"You won the Vanguard Teacher Award?" Alberta asked.

"Professor von Offel actually gave you a positive recommendation?" Prescott added.

The bell rang, and in strode the professor, followed by his parrot, Atom.

"Then what are *they* still doing here?" Luis whispered.

"Oh, this isn't the Vanguard Teacher Award!" Dr. Kepler held up the gold-edged certificate, then smiled at the professor. "The Third Millennium

Foundation isn't the only group interested in our star science teacher."

The professor yawned.

The principal's smile grew wider. "Of course, it *is* the most prestigious."

The professor's yawn grew larger.

Alberta's hand shot up. "What kind of grant is it?"

"And will there be an awards banquet?" Sean Baxter added. "Something with a dessert buffet?"

The principal laughed. "I'm afraid this is as close to an awards ceremony as we'll get." She handed the certificate to Mr. Flask and shook his hand. Then she turned back to the class. "As for dessert, if you'd like, I could have the cafeteria send over a vat of their famous rice pudding."

The room erupted in groans.

Sean wrinkled his nose. "No, thanks."

"Then maybe Mr. Flask would like to move on to his acceptance speech?" Dr. Kepler said.

The teacher smiled and stepped forward. "On behalf of the Arcana Parks Department and Einstein Elementary, I'd like to thank the government for this environmental education grant. The money will allow us to build a footbridge over the stream that separates our school property from the Arcana Nature Preserve."

"Excellent," Sean called out. "Pass the field trip permission slips!"

"And since the city has already approved the bridge design," the teacher continued, "the Parks

Department can begin construction right away. The grant will also allow us to fix up the preserve's historic fire tower, which has been closed to the public for many years. Once it's reopened, classes will be able to use the tower for all kinds of lessons. For instance, think what a bird's-eye view will do for our study of trees!"

"Wait," Heather Patterson said. "Isn't that the really tall, crooked tower?"

Mr. Flask glanced back at the professor and colored slightly. "No, you're thinking of the old von Offel tower, built in 1891. The one we'll be refurbishing was built the previous year by my ancestor, Jedidiah Flask."

The professor frowned. "And what's wrong with the old von Offel tower?" he demanded.

"Don't get me wrong," the teacher said. "It would have been a great achievement if it had been finished. But somehow they never got around to adding cross bracing, which is odd, since most crews would have put that in place as they built."

"Stuff and nonsense!" the professor fumed. "Of course the tower is finished. We intentionally omitted the cross bracing."

Dr. Kepler gave the professor a curious look.

Max Hoof thrust his hand into the air. "What do you mean 'we,' Professor? You weren't alive in 1891 — or were you?"

Prescott's eyes widened. Would Max succeed in exposing the professor as a ghost — and accidentally ruin Mr. Flask's shot at winning the Vanguard Teacher Award?

Mr. Flask just laughed. "When the professor said 'we,' he meant the von Offel family. Max, you of all people should know how wrapped up people get in their ancestors' stories. Your mother is the president of the Daughters of Arcana. Every Founder's Day, she dresses up like her ancestor Felicia Smutton and helps reenact the crossing of the Arcana River."

Max slumped down in his seat. "Yeah, and she makes me dress up like Felicia's klutzy son, Percy, the first settler to fall into the Arcana River."

The professor cleared his throat impatiently. "The von Offel tower is taller. Therefore it is better. I demand it be preserved!"

"With all due respect, Professor," Mr. Flask said, "I just can't agree. The von Offel tower wouldn't be the safest, strongest tower for us to use."

"It's made of steel, just like the Flask tower," the professor said. "Why wouldn't it be just as strong?"

"Steel *is* strong," the teacher agreed. "But when you're building, the form — or shape — of your structure is just as important as the material you use."

The professor pushed back from his desk and strode to the chalkboard at the front of the room. "We used good solid squares and rectangles," he said, drawing the shapes as he spoke. He tapped the board with the chalk. "I defy you to show me something stronger!"

Mr. Flask opened his mouth to reply. Then he paused and looked over at Dr. Kepler.

The principal was deep in thought: If Mr. Flask made Professor von Offel look bad, the professor might not give a favorable recommendation of him to the Third Millennium Foundation. On the other hand, Mr. Flask couldn't allow the professor to mislead his students. Some things were more important than awards. The principal cleared her throat. "Yes, Mr. Flask," she said. "The professor has shown us two strong shapes. Can you show us a stronger one?"

Mr. Flask smiled and picked up a piece of chalk. First he drew a square. Then he added a line from corner to corner, as if he were cutting a sandwich. Finally, he added a second line between the other two corners.

"See? That's clearly a square," the professor said. "It just has that fussy cross bracing inside."

"That cross bracing breaks this square up into four triangles," Mr. Flask said. "And a triangle is a more stable shape than a square or any other rectangle."

"Balderdash!" the professor exclaimed. "You'll never prove that."

"Here's one quick way to see what I mean," the teacher said. "Everyone put your right hand on your left elbow and your left hand on your right elbow. Look down. You've just formed a rectangle. Its four sides are your right upper arm, your chest, your left upper arm, and your right and left lower arms together."

Luis looked down at his arms and nodded.

"To keep things stable, make sure your shoulders stay pressed against the back of your chair," Mr. Flask continued. "Now keep your hands in place, but try to change the rectangle's shape."

Alberta shifted her left elbow over a few inches. "Hey, I made a — what would you call this?" Alberta lifted her arms for the teacher to see.

"A parallelogram," Mr. Flask replied. "That's a four-sided shape whose opposite sides are parallel and the same length. A diamond is one kind of parallelogram."

Alberta shifted her arms from side to side. "Hey, I can make it a fat parallelogram or a skinny one."

The teacher nodded. "Rectangles can be" — he glanced at the scowling professor — "very *flexible*."

"I haven't seen your almighty triangle perform yet," the professor sniffed.

"Fair enough," Mr. Flask said. "Okay, everybody drop your arms to your sides. Now put your right hand on your left shoulder. You've just made a triangle whose three sides are your lower arm, your upper arm, and your chest. Try to change the shape of that triangle. Just remember to keep your hand planted firmly on your shoulder and your back pressed against your chair."

Alberta concentrated hard. "Hey, I can't even

budge it," she said. She switched her arms back to the rectangle and shifted the shape back and forth. "What an incredible difference!"

"I cry foul!" the professor said. "This young lady's arms are nothing like the strong steel girders in the majestic von Offel tower. Towers have rivets to hold the steel beams steady. Their joints don't swing freely like elbows and shoulders."

"Rivets do lend *some* stability to a tower's joints — the places where one piece of steel meets another," Mr. Flask said. "But for safety's sake, engineers can't count on rivets to keep a joint from moving, well — like an elbow. So shape is important. And triangles, as you just experienced, are a very stable shape. That's why most steel structures use triangles as part of their design."

The professor's eyes narrowed. "By your logic, Flask, the magnificent von Offel tower should be —"

"Bravo, gentlemen!" Dr. Kepler interrupted the professor with brisk applause. "This has been a very interesting lesson. Nothing illuminates a scientific principle like a spirited debate. Mr. Flask, I hope you'll take this opportunity to begin a unit on the science of structures."

The professor grunted. "Just how many lessons do you think he can teach on the alleged superiority of the triangle?"

"Oh, I'm sure that's not all there is to the science of structures," Dr. Kepler said, looking meaningfully at Mr. Flask.

"Of course not," Mr. Flask said. "In fact, I promise not to mention triangles again today."

The professor stalked back to his desk and picked up his quill pen. "We'll just see about that, won't we?"

Atom was teetering on his brass perch, swaying back and forth as he struggled to place his right wing tip on his left shoulder.

"Do you mind?" von Offel hissed.

"Just reaching for an itch!" the parrot blurted out.

The professor clamped Atom's beak shut with his fingers.

"Sometimes that parrot sounds almost human," Dr. Kepler marveled. "A bird that smart must be priceless."

The professor bared his teeth in a smile and looked at Atom. "Priceless — worthless, sometimes one wonders."

"I see." The principal paused. "Well, I'll leave you gentlemen and students to your studies. Ethan, I'll call the Parks Department and tell them they can start work anytime." She gave the class one last smile, then walked out the door.

CHAPTER 2

Tumbling Toothpicks

M r. Flask rummaged around a lab supply cabinet and pulled out a large hunk of modeling clay and some boxes of round toothpicks. He handed them to Prescott, who began passing them out. "Use these materials to build the highest tower possible," the teacher said. He pinched off a piece of Alberta's lump of clay and stuck two toothpicks into it. "By the way," he added, "in case you want to try this at home later, you can also do it with toothpicks and gumdrops."

"Gumdrops!" Sean said, frowning at his clay. "I don't know, Mr. Flask. Looks like another student-pleasing opportunity lost." He glanced back at Professor von Offel. "You know, this could affect your chances of winning that award if the professor's foundation asks for student recommendations."

The teacher laughed. "Well, I wouldn't want to win under false pretenses, Sean. You'll just have to tell the truth."

Sean shrugged and pinched off a small piece of

clay. He stuck it to his desk and poked a toothpick into it. He topped it with a second lump of clay and a second toothpick. Then a third set of each. Then a fourth. "This is easy!" Sean said. He looked over at Alberta, who was carefully putting together a cube. "Mine is already four times higher than yours," he laughed. "You have to build boldly!"

"My sentiment exactly," said the professor, his eyes scanning the room.

Mr. Flask laughed. "That's a fast way to build, and it saves on materials. But I'm afraid you'll see its limitations soon."

"Besides, how could someone climb it?" Alberta said. "There's no place to put stairs."

Sean added a fifth lump of clay and toothpick. "This is an extreme climbing tower. You have to shimmy up it." He took a lump of clay and pressed it to the side of the top toothpick. "See, here's me climbing my way to victory." As soon as he let go, the tower, unbalanced by the lump of clay, keeled over.

Alberta laughed softly.

"Hey, I meant to do that," Sean protested. "After you finish the extreme climb, you get to do the extreme tower dive."

Prescott was finishing up his third story. His tower looked like a stack of three cubes. "I have to admit that I see why Professor von Offel chose squares for his tower," he said to Alberta. "They're easy, and they seem strong enough so far."

Alberta was finishing her fourth story. "They definitely are easy."

Sean edged his desk closer to Luis's. "What are you doing? You haven't even gotten a single story yet."

"Mr. Flask showed us that triangles are stronger than squares," Luis said. "I'm going to build my tower with triangles — if I can figure out how."

At the sound of the word *triangles*, the professor froze. "Flask!"

The teacher smiled and shrugged. "I promised *I* wouldn't say the word, but I can't stifle my students' creativity."

Professor von Offel pushed himself out of his seat and walked over to Alberta's desk. "Look at this elegant tower," he said. "It's six stories already and standing straight as a — well, it's *standing*, at any rate."

Alberta reached up to begin the seventh story. "It's getting kind of shaky, though. I keep having to go back and straighten up my lower stories." She added a few more toothpicks and sat back to admire her seven-story tower. "I guess I might climb it — if it were made of steel."

"Don't look now, but your tower's sagging," Sean laughed.

Alberta watched in dismay as her tower listed slowly to the right, then suddenly broke and toppled. "It was fine a minute ago," she said. "What made it fall over?"

"Don't worry, Alberta," Mr. Flask said. "The history of building is full of structures that seemed fine one minute and collapsed the next."

Prescott looked up at the ceiling. "Is that supposed to make her feel better?" he asked. "It kind of makes me want to go running out into an open field."

Mr. Flask laughed. "Luckily, engineers learned from each of those catastrophic failures and ultimately built safer buildings because of them."

Sean pointed at Alberta's heap of toothpicks and clay. "So what's the lesson of that? Gravity rules?"

The teacher smiled. "That's part of it. When a structure is made of squares, a lot of the load is carried by the joints. Even though Alberta's tower didn't have a person or vehicle on it — what engineers call a *live load* — it did have to support the weight of its own building materials — what engineers call its *dead load*. It started out a little unbalanced just because it's a tower made by hand of toothpicks and clay. As gravity pulled down on the dead load, the tower kept shifting, becoming more and more unevenly balanced. Finally, the distortion was too much. One joint failed. That shifted the load to another joint, which wasn't designed to handle the extra force. The second joint quickly failed, then another, then another, until Alberta's whole structure was flat on the ground."

Alberta looked over at Prescott, who was finishing up his sixth story. His tower shifted abruptly, and he caught it in his hands.

"Looks like I'm not even going to make it to the seventh story," Prescott said. He tried to adjust the tower's balance but finally gave up and let it topple.

"Hey, look at Luis's," Alberta said.

Luis was patiently building a four-sided building whose sides were made of equilateral triangles, or triangles with sides of equal length.

"How did you do that?" Prescott asked.

"I just messed around until I got it," Luis said. "I had to break some toothpicks to get it flat on the bottom. But now it's going pretty smoothly."

"Mr. Flask, is that what the fire tower looks like?" Alberta asked.

"No," the teacher said. "The fire tower is more like your design, only with X-shaped cross bracing inside each square. Luis's tower reminds me of the Bank of China building in Hong Kong. I'm impressed."

Luis smiled and kept building.

The professor frowned. "That's all well and good, but it's taking him forever to build. On top of that, he's using a lot more toothpicks than the other students are. It's criminal waste!"

"But look how much sturdier his tower is," Alberta said. "It's not sagging at all. I'd climb that one any day."

"But are we all going to stand around and wait for

him?" von Offel said. "I, for one, have better things to do." He leaned over Luis's desk. "Boy, just start stacking squares on top of that, and you'll be done in two shakes of a lamb's tail."

"Yeah," Prescott whispered to Alberta. "Because it'll topple over."

Mr. Flask went back to the science closet and pulled out a large jar of pennies and a bag of plastic clips. "While Luis is finishing his tower, everyone else can explore another building material — coins and coin connectors. Let's see how high a tower you can build out of these."

The professor slammed his office door behind him. "I didn't work hard building the von Offel tower just to have Arcana cast it aside like an old shoe!"

"Darn right, you didn't work hard building that tower," Atom said, launching himself off the professor's shoulder and landing on the desk. "As I remember, at the time you bragged insufferably about how little work you put into it. All you could talk about were the steps you skipped, the corners you cut —"

"All part of the proud von Offel work ethic," von Offel insisted.

"The von Offel work ethic?" Atom said. "This ought to be good."

"A von Offel's overriding goal is no wasted effort," the professor explained. "Where a Flask might

14

say, 'Measure twice, cut once,' a von Offel says, 'Hey, Flask, would you mind cutting this for me?'"

The bird laughed. "Or how about, 'Hey, Atom, fly over and see whether Flask has some of these already cut'?"

"You remember!" the professor said warmly. "So you can see why I'm so distressed that my efforts, however curtailed, might go to waste. I just don't understand why Arcana would pick Flask's puny tower over mine!"

"Common sense?" Atom said. "Public safety?"

"You may be right," the professor said thoughtfully. "And if that's all it is, we may still have a chance to save the von Offel tower." He reached into his desk and pulled out a piece of parchment and a quill pen. "I'm hatching a plan. And as with all good von Offel plans, I'm bringing in someone else to do the work."

CHAPTER 3

An Anonymous Tip

When the sixth graders arrived at the science lab the next day, Professor von Offel was already at his desk, his hands folded. Atom stood on his perch as still as a statue.

"That's weird," Luis whispered. "When was the last time they were here before the bell rang?"

Alberta slipped into her chair. "The professor seems really interested in the structures unit," she reasoned. "Maybe he didn't want to miss anything."

Prescott made a face. "He was only interested yesterday because he was trying to prove that the von Offel tower wasn't a dangerous heap of junk," he said. "And he failed big time, I might add."

The bell rang. Behind the lab assistants, someone gasped loudly. The three spun around and saw Max, his face distorted in a mask of pure shock and terror. "Mother?" he mouthed. He sank down in his seat until his nose nearly touched his desk.

"Mr. Flask, I demand a word with you." Max's

mother marched across the room and waved a piece of paper in the teacher's face.

Mr. Flask looked down at the paper. "If this is about the lab assistant thing again," he said quietly, "another time would be —"

"As you may know, I'm the president of the Daughters of Arcana," Mrs. Hoof interrupted.

The teacher nodded. "Of course."

"It's our mission to keep the history of Arcana alive and to preserve its historic landmarks."

Mr. Flask smiled. "Yes, we have an Arcana landmark plaque on the Flask mansion."

"Then you should know better!" Max's mother thundered.

"What is this about?" the teacher asked.

Mrs. Hoof shook the sheet of paper in her hand. "An anonymous community watchdog has alerted me to the fact that you are planning to tear down the von Offel tower!"

The teacher took a deep breath. "I don't know where your *watchdog* got his or her information. But there seems to be a misunderstanding."

"I doubt it," Max's mother said. "My anonymous champion of Arcana's history is obviously a man — or woman — of culture. I've studied enough old documents to know that this letter was written on parchment with a quill pen. That's a skill most of us have regrettably lost."

Luis rolled his eyes. "Yeah, like more than a century ago when everybody started using fountain pens," he whispered to Alberta.

The professor stood up. "I'm something of a quill pen aficionado myself, dear lady. May I see your document?"

Max barely stifled another gasp of horror.

His mother sailed past his desk without even noticing him. Her eyes were fixed on the professor. "Why, thank you, sir." She half curtsied as she handed him the parchment.

The professor pulled out his monocle. Mrs. Hoof's hand fluttered to her chest.

"Indeed, madam, this was undoubtedly written with a quill pen," von Offel said, handing the paper back to her. "And with a very distinguished hand, I might add. How cultured of you to know."

Mrs. Hoof colored slightly. "*Cultured* was just the word that came to my mind when I saw that magnificent suit," she said. "I've never seen such authentic-looking 19th-century haberdashery outside of a museum."

"Why, I have a whole trunkful of these suits over at the von Offel mansion."

"Then you're Professor John von Offel?" Mrs. Hoof said. "Why, I was going to try to track you down this very afternoon in hopes that you would join our crusade to save the von Offel tower."

The professor took her hand and cupped it in both of his. "Then it seems our meeting was written in the stars. I'd be honored to join your gallant movement, if you think I could help."

At the front of the classroom, Mr. Flask cleared his throat. "Pardon me for interrupting, Mrs. Hoof, but I have to set the record straight. I don't have any plans to destroy the von Offel tower. In fact, I don't have any plans for the von Offel tower at all. Our grant includes funds for two projects: the construction of a bridge between the school property and the Arcana Nature Preserve, and the restoration of the old fire tower."

Mrs. Hoof narrowed her eyes. "So it's true that you didn't request any funding to repair the von Offel tower?"

"Well, no, because —"

"Neglect is a hairbreadth from destruction!" Mrs. Hoof said. "I demand that some of that grant money be used to preserve the von Offel tower. After all, it has historic value." She tapped her finger on the parchment. "It's the largest tower in the state built without cross bracing!"

"But surely you can see that —" the teacher began.

Professor von Offel cut him off. "If you check the historic records, dear lady, I believe that you'll find some other superlatives as well. For a tower of its height and date, it had the lowest budget as well as the fastest completion time. You'll also find no record of any injuries."

"No injuries in a construction project that large!" Mrs. Hoof marveled.

The professor nodded happily. "No *record* whatsoever. No matter how hard you look." He put his finger in the air. "Ah, that reminds me. It's not well known, but your son's ancestor, Smedley Hoof, made his own contributions to the project."

"Oh?" Max's mother said, her eyes growing wide.

"As a government official, he helped grease the works to get the project approved. You might say the project couldn't have been built without him!"

"How marvelous!" Mrs. Hoof said. "Every scrap of family history that I can gather for Max is like a precious jewel. I do hope you'll let me pick your brain."

The professor drew back in horror. "I beg your pardon?"

The color drained from Mrs. Hoof's face. "No, I beg *your* pardon," she said. "That was clumsily put. I meant I would love to discuss Arcana's rich history with you someday."

"It's a day I look forward to," the professor said, bowing.

Max sank lower in his seat.

Mrs. Hoof turned back to the teacher. "So, now that you understand its historic importance to Arcana, do you agree to preserve the grand von Offel tower?"

Mr. Flask sighed. "Naturally, I'd love to help you with your efforts. But I'm afraid there's no extra money in the grant."

"But surely you padded your budget," Mrs. Hoof said. "If nothing else, history teaches that."

The professor nodded solemnly.

"No, the budget is very bare bones," Mr. Flask said. "It covers materials only. All of the labor will be done by the Parks Department."

Mrs. Hoof straightened her back and glared at him. "Are you refusing my official request, made on behalf of the Daughters of Arcana, to preserve the von Offel tower?"

Mr. Flask frowned. "That's not the way I would have put it, but I suppose the answer is yes."

Mrs. Hoof waved the parchment in the air. "I have not yet begun to fight!" She strode to the door and searched the class for Max. "Stop slouching, dear!" she added. Then she turned on her heel and walked through the door.

Max sank lower, then disappeared completely beneath his desk.

CHAPTER 4

Max Under Tension — and Compression

M r. Flask walked down the aisle toward Max's desk. "Are you okay?" He reached out and helped Max to his feet.

Max's cheeks were bright pink. "She's just so forceful," he said. "I feel pushed and pulled, pushed and pulled. I'm under such pressure." He looked around, embarrassed at his outbreak.

Mr. Flask put a hand on his shoulder. "It sounds like you know just what a building feels like. Thanks for introducing our topic for today."

Max looked puzzled.

"Come up front and help me demonstrate," Mr. Flask said. "If you're up to it," he added gently.

Max nodded and followed the teacher.

"Buildings are designed to support heavy loads," Mr. Flask began. "Civil engineers — people who make sure that structures are strong enough — divide the loads into different categories. The first is dead load, which I mentioned yesterday. A building's dead load is its own weight. Max, if you were a building, what would the weight of your dead load be?"

Max thought for a moment. "I guess it would be the same as my body weight — about 75 pounds."

Alberta raised her hand. "Why do engineers even worry about dead load? Can't *every* building automatically hold up its own weight? I mean, heavier things are stronger, right? The more stuff you add to something, the stronger it gets, and so — oh, wait."

Mr. Flask smiled. "Thinking about our clay and toothpick towers yesterday?" he asked.

Alberta nodded.

"Each time you added a toothpick or lump of clay to your tower, you were adding to its dead load. When your tower was four stories, it was strong enough to bear the dead load. But when it was seven stories —"

"Ka-plooeey!" Sean said.

The teacher smiled. "The next kind of load is live load, the weight of the additional stuff a structure needs to hold up. For a skyscraper, that means furniture and people. For a bridge, that means pedestrians, bikes, cars, or even trains." He turned to Max. "So, what makes up your live load, Max?"

Max looked down. "My clothes?"

"That's an important one," Mr. Flask said. "What else do you need to carry?"

Max looked around. "My backpack, a book, a pencil, a lunch tray —"

Mr. Flask nodded. "A person's live load changes a lot over the day. Okay, let's think about buildings again. A building's load is expressed in pounds per square foot. Basically, the engineers take the number of pounds they need a structure to hold and divide it by the number of square feet. Suppose you know your structure will usually have, say, 100 pounds per square foot. Would you design it to withstand exactly that much load?"

Luis raised his hand. "Wouldn't you want to build it stronger, in case something unusual happened? Like, what if they had a big party? Or they were a business and got in a huge shipment of something?"

"Good point," Mr. Flask said. "You want to stay on the safe side. You don't want your structure to cave in if you happen to reach 101 pounds per square foot. So would you build it to withstand, say, 1,000 pounds per square foot?"

"Why not?" Sean said. "It could be like a super-buff bodybuilding building."

"That seems like overkill," Alberta said. "It must cost extra money to make a building stronger."

The teacher nodded. "It does. So engineers strive to make a building stronger than it ever needs to be, without wasting money by making it inappropriately strong."

Prescott looked up and raised his hand. "That ceiling looks like a pretty heavy dead load. How did the people who built this school know that the building could hold it up — and keep holding it up, even if it's covered with a live load, like, I don't know, birds?"

Sean laughed. "You really think engineers worry about birds? No offense to Mr. Flask, but no one with a real job spends a single second thinking about birds."

In the back of the classroom, Atom squawked indignantly.

Mr. Flask laughed. "I'm not offended, Sean, but I bet there are a lot of ornithologists who would disagree."

"Okay, how about snow, then?" Prescott asked. "I've shoveled enough to know it's pretty heavy."

"Over the years, engineers and scientists have collected a lot of data about the strength of building materials, the annual snowfall in different parts of the country, and so on," the teacher explained. "So when an engineer starts to build a structure, she or he looks up all of that stuff and factors it into the design."

In the back of the class, the professor snorted. "That's if you're a Flask, you do. How utterly boring. Where's the room for creativity and innovation?"

Mr. Flask laughed. "There's room for both, so long as you follow the building codes — which are really based on the unshakable laws of physics."

The professor snorted again.

"Neither dead nor live loads change very quickly," Mr. Flask continued. "But one of the hottest areas for engineering innovation is in designing buildings to withstand unpredictable forces like high winds or earthquakes. Either one can place a sudden, changing force on a building that can cause great damage."

Prescott looked back up at the ceiling. "Is this building designed to withstand earthquakes?"

"We're not in a part of the country that has many earthquakes," Mr. Flask said. "So engineers wouldn't have had to take that into account." Mr. Flask picked a dictionary off the shelf and laid it gently on Max's head. "Let's go back to the dead and live loads, which they *did* factor in. Do these loads push or pull on a structure?"

"Push," the class answered in unison.

"Wait," Prescott said. "I can see where the desks and people would push down on the floor. But wouldn't the light fixtures pull on the ceiling?"

Mr. Flask smiled and tucked the book back into the bookcase. "Nice observation, Prescott. But that's only a small part of it. In fact, every structure is subject to both pushes *and* pulls. Engineers call these forces *compression* and *tension*. Compression — the pushing — may be a little easier to imagine." He rummaged under a lab sink and pulled out a thick cellulose kitchen sponge. He ran the sponge under the tap to soften in, then squeezed it out and carried it to the front of the classroom. "Say that Max is a column holding up a ceiling. The weight of the ceiling puts compression on him." Mr. Flask put his hand on Max's head and pushed down gently. "Compression makes things shorter, like this." He held the sponge vertically and pushed down on it.

"You made me shorter?" Max sighed. "Great. That's all I need."

Mr. Flask laughed. "It was only temporary. As soon as I lifted the load, you returned to your regular height, like this." He took his hand off Max and off the sponge, which quickly stretched back into shape.

Mr. Flask pulled up two chairs and positioned them about 20 inches apart. "Max, could you lie facedown across these two chairs? Everything between your knees and your chest should be suspended in the middle."

Max nodded reluctantly.

When Max was in place, Mr. Flask faced the class. "Now, think of the chairs as columns and Max's body as a beam between them. Is Max's body being pushed or pulled?"

The class was silent.

"It doesn't seem like either one," Alberta said.

"What do *you* say, Max?" Mr. Flask said.

"Well, I don't feel pushed *or* pulled," Max said. "If anything, I'm just sagging a little bit."

Mr. Flask motioned for Max to stand up. "That sagging actually causes both compression and tension." He held up the sponge and bent it into a U shape. He carried it from desk to desk. "See the wrinkles along the top edge? The top surface is under compression — it's being pushed and shortened. Meanwhile, the bottom surface of the sponge is under tension — it's being pulled and stretched. If you measured both surfaces, the bottom edge would actually be longer. The same would be true for a steel beam, though the difference in length would be much, much smaller. You probably couldn't measure it without a special instrument called a *strain gauge*."

Max's eyes flicked toward the doorway where he'd last seen his mother. "If you put a strain gauge on me," he muttered, "my reading would probably be off the charts."

After class, Prescott collared Luis and Alberta right outside the door. "Do you think Mr. Flask realizes that the professor sent that letter to Mrs. Hoof?"

"Who else in this town, in this nation even, writes with a quill pen?" Alberta asked.

"It just seems like Mr. Flask doesn't want to believe anything bad about the professor," Prescott said. "Like that he's a mean-spirited, conniving ghost."

"Mr. Flask doesn't believe the professor is a ghost because that idea violates the rules of science," Luis said. "But there's nothing unscientific about a cranky old guy writing a protest letter. He won't have any trouble believing that."

Max stuck his head out of the lab door. "You haven't seen my mom out there, have you?" he asked the lab assistants.

Alberta shook her head. "The coast is clear."

Max sighed and stepped into the hallway.

"Is your mom really going to stop Mr. Flask from building the bridge and saving the fire tower?" Prescott asked him.

Max shrugged. "If she says she will, she probably will. I'm more worried about her and the ghost."

Alberta glanced at Prescott. "What ghost?" she asked Max innocently.

"You know exactly who I mean!" Max said, his voice rising to a whiny peak. "What if my mom marries him? I could never sleep with a ghost in the house."

"Marries him?" Luis said. "They met less than an hour ago!"

"It never hurts to worry ahead," Max said. "It saves time later."

"You know," Prescott said, "if your mom really *is* interested in the professor, you'd probably better drop this stuff about his being a ghost."

Max threw up his hands. "Actually, that would give me all the more reason to expose the professor and save my mother from him!" His eyes suddenly widened. "Unless she'd be *more* interested in him when she found out he was a ghost. He probably knows a lot of Arcana history —"

Luis rolled his eyes. "I really think you're jumping the gun here, Max. They talked for about 30 seconds."

Max crossed his arms. "Well, whether or not my mom likes the professor, I'm going to prove he's a ghost." He stomped off down the hall.

The lab assistants walked toward their next class.

"What are we going to do about Max?" Prescott asked. "He seems more determined than ever."

"Let's just keep an eye on him," Alberta said. "Even if he came up with some real evidence, Mr. Flask is too busy to consider it."

"And even if he managed to convince his mother," Luis added, "I'm not so sure that any sane, reasonable adult would believe her."

CHAPTER 5

Árches and I Beams

Mrs. Hoof tapped the blackboard with a piece of chalk. "I've found the needed funds for saving the von Offel tower!" she announced as class began the next day.

Sean scanned the detailed footbridge drawing that Max's mother had copied onto the board. "There was money buried under the bridge? But I thought it wasn't even finished yet."

"They finished the foundations yesterday — one on each side of the river," Mr. Flask said. "Tomorrow they'll start building between them. First they'll lay the two steel beams across the river. Then they'll make a floor of wooden six-by-sixes between them. Finally, they'll add handrails."

"Excellent!" Mrs. Hoof said. "Then I'm not too late to bring this to a satisfying conclusion."

"What do you have in mind?" the teacher asked warily.

Mrs. Hoof tapped the board again, indicating the bottom of the bridge. "Steel beams seem extravagant. Surely you could build the entire bridge out of wood. Our ancestors spanned plenty of rivers before they invented steel." She smiled and inclined her head toward the professor. "The money you save could go toward preserving the historic von Offel tower."

The professor returned her smile. "A brilliant solution, madam. Thank you."

Mrs. Hoof blushed happily.

"Well, we could build the entire bridge out of wood," Mr. Flask agreed. "But it would end up costing us *more* money, not less."

"Wooden two-by-fours more expensive than steel beams?" exclaimed Mrs. Hoof. "How could that be?"

"Steel is stronger than wood," Mr. Flask explained. "A single steel beam may be more expensive than a plank of wood. But it can support a lot more weight, so you don't need as much of it. If we used wood, we'd have to build an arch under the bridge in order to make it strong enough. Not only would that use extra wood, it would be more complicated and time-consuming to build."

Alberta raised her hand. "An arch is kind of a half circle, right? How would that help support the bridge?"

Mr. Flask pulled some books off a shelf and made two equal stacks on his desk about four inches tall and six inches apart. He laid a sheet of paper between them like a bridge, then a second sheet of paper on top of that. "How many pennies do you think these two pieces of paper can hold?" he asked.

Prescott raised his hand. "Paper is pretty flimsy. Maybe one?"

The teacher brought out his jar of pennies and motioned for Prescott to come forward.

Prescott put one penny in the middle of the paper, then two. When he added a third, the two sheets of paper buckled and slid between the books. "Two pennies," Prescott said. "I was close."

Mr. Flask dropped the pennies back into the jar and picked up the two pieces of paper. He curved one into an upside-down U and placed it between the two stacks of books. Then he put the second piece of paper back in place on top of the two books. The papers now formed a bridge supported by an arch. "How many pennies can the two pieces of paper support now?" he asked.

Alberta raised her hand. "If the other bridge held two, maybe four?"

The teacher handed her the jar of pennies.

Alberta carefully added penny after penny, making sure to keep the load balanced. The bridge finally collapsed under the weight of 12 pennies. "It held 11 pennies. That's more than five times as strong as before!" Alberta said.

Mrs. Hoof scowled. "Very little good that does us, since it's more expensive." She leaned closer to her own drawing. "Your blueprints indicated that these steel beams aren't completely solid."

Mr. Flask nodded. "They're called I beams. If you look at one from the end, it looks like a capital letter

I." He laid a book flat on his desk and stood a second book upright on the middle of it. Then he held a third book horizontally and balanced it on top. "Here's what it looks like, only a lot longer."

Mrs. Hoof walked over to the books. "To use your model," she said, "the top book would be holding up the wooden planks. That's important. But the bottom book is simply resting on the foundation, and the middle book is just sitting between them. It seems clear to me that you really need only the top book. So why not just use a single strip of steel? That would surely save money."

In the back of the classroom, the professor applauded briskly. "Bravo, madam. I do believe you've rescued us this time!"

Mrs. Hoof smiled and aimed a small curtsy at the professor. "You're too kind, sir." She turned toward Mr. Flask, and her smile faded. "Particularly since we haven't yet heard from the teacher."

"In the face of such impeccable logic, even young Flask must submit to your will," the professor said. "And if he has any taste, he'll consider it an honor."

Max's mother lowered her eyes demurely.

Mr. Flask took a deep breath. "I appreciate Mrs. Hoof's suggestion," he began. "However, maybe this is a good time for me to explain how an I beam works. Long ago, engineers noticed that the top surface of any beam is in compression, while the bottom surface is in tension."

"Like the sponge you bent yesterday," Alberta said.

"And like Max lying between the chairs!" Sean added.

Mrs. Hoof's eyebrows went up.

"Just a little demonstration Max helped me with," Mr. Flask assured her. He turned back to the class. "The engineers realized that a beam's top and bottom surfaces do the real support work. The middle part, they found, doesn't support nearly as much. Its main job is to hold the top and bottom surfaces the right distance apart. The engineers theorized that it would be better to make the top and bottom surfaces really wide and the middle relatively skinny. The result was the I beam, which turns out to be a very economical shape. It's nearly as strong as a solid steel beam the same overall size. But there's a lot less steel in it, which makes it lighter *and* cheaper."

Mrs. Hoof's lips pursed in frustration. She searched her chalkboard drawing for another money-saving idea.

Mr. Flask picked up the two pieces of paper, which were still between the stacks of books. "Another way to understand why I beams work is to consider the extra strength that folds can give a surface." He lined up the two pieces of paper and folded them lengthwise, like an accordion or paper fan. When he turned the edge toward the class, Prescott thought it looked like two W's strung together. The teacher then laid the paper between the two stacks of books, with the folds running from one stack to the other. "How many pennies do you think these two pieces of paper can hold now?" Mr. Flask asked.

Luis raised his hand. "Seems like there would have to be a lot of weight there to bend those folds," he predicted. "Maybe 30?"

Mr. Flask handed Luis the penny jar.

Luis counted out 10 pennies, then 20, then 30, then 40. "It still hardly shows signs of stress," he marveled. He upped the count to 50, 60, 70. A few minutes later, he was still counting. "That's 150 and still holding," he said.

"You can stop there," Mr. Flask said. "I think you get the point."

Luis sat down, a little stunned. "Yeah, it's more than 75 times stronger than the original paper bridge."

Alberta raised her hand, her eyes on the huge pile of pennies. "If I'm going to be walking across that bridge, I vote we keep the steel I beam, with its nice strong folds."

Mrs. Hoof crossed her arms. "This is not over," she declared. She looked back at the professor and poked her finger into the air. "Don't give up hope, dear sir!" she assured him. Then she looked around for Max. "Darling," she said, "don't forget your ballroom-dancing lessons this afternoon!" And with that, she stalked out of the classroom.

"Ballroom-dancing lessons?" Sean laughed. "What kind of loser takes ballroom-dancing lessons?"

Max slid down in his seat.

"*I'm* in Max's ballroom-dancing class," Heather announced icily.

Sean tried hard not to look embarrassed. Every other boy in the class was regarding Max with a look of envy and awe.

"You get to dance with *Heather*?" Prescott breathed. "Every week?"

Mr. Flask suppressed a grin.

Alberta rolled her eyes. Then she raised her hand. "If nobody minds my changing the subject back to *science*," she said. "That folded paper bridge is strong, but I kind of liked the paper arch bridge. It was, well, pretty."

The teacher nodded. "I agree. And it's the perfect shape for today's cool, building experiment material. Everybody team up with two other people."

Mr. Flask brought out a bag of brightly colored packing pellets and handed them to Luis to pass out. "These look a lot like Styrofoam, but they're made of cornstarch, so they're better for the environment. Some people use them for cushioning packages, but they're also fun to build with."

Mr. Flask moistened a paper towel and touched it to the end of a pink cornstarch pellet. He pressed the moist end of the pink pellet against a green pellet, and the two pieces stuck together.

"Neat," Alberta said. "How does it work?"

Mr. Flask handed her some moist paper towels to pass out. "If you drop one of these cornstarch pellets into water, it will dissolve," he said. "But if you just dab the foam with water, it gets a little gooey instead. Stick the gooey end to another pellet, and the two pieces cling together. When the water evaporates, it leaves behind a nice, strong bond." He looked around to make sure each group had its materials. "Okay, today I'd like you to make a bridge out of these cornstarch pellets. You can make a flat bridge, an arch bridge, or even one with an I beam shape. Just use your imagination!"

Sean connected a long line of cornstarch pellets and hung them between two desks. He turned to Max. "Hey, Fred Astaire! Maybe Mr. Flask should build the bridge out of these," he said. "Think that would make your mom happy?"

Max looked back at the professor, who was building a crooked tower out of pellets. "I don't think I even want to know what would make my mom happy," he said.

CHAPTER 6

Edible? Doubtable!

The next morning, the lab assistants showed up early to feed the classroom animals.

Mr. Flask was whistling as he let them into the science lab. "The parks crew starts constructing the bridge this morning," he reminded them.

Luis sprinkled flakes into the aquariums. Alberta poured some mealworms into the turtle habitat.

Prescott filled a water bottle and reattached it to the hamster habitat. He pointed to the fluffy rodent burrowed under the cedar chips. "Hey, I just thought of something. This cage isn't really Lightning Bolt's home. That hole under the wood chips is. I mean, that's where he goes to sleep every morning, right?"

Mr. Flask smiled. "Great observation! He spends the night roaming the whole cage like it's a mini habitat. But when he's ready to sleep, he comes back to that same corner and makes a cozy little bedroom under the cedar chips."

Lightning Bolt poked a sleepy nose out of his

hole. Prescott laughed. "He doesn't have to worry about his cedar-chip ceiling falling down. It sits right on his back."

"Sounds like Grace," Alberta said, lifting up a box turtle.

Mr. Flask laughed. "We do talk about turtles carrying their homes on their backs. But a lot of turtles, including Grace, burrow under the ground when they sleep. Some dig in wherever they are, and some make deeper, sturdier burrows that they come back to over and over."

Prescott glanced over at Luis's toothpick-and-clay tower, which was standing on a counter. "Digging is one thing," he said. "But do any animals really *build* structures, like people do?"

"How about bird nests?" Alberta said.

"I was thinking of something more impressive," Prescott said. "Bird nests are just some sticks stuck together."

Alberta pointed to Luis's toothpick tower. "What do you think that is?"

"Well, Luis's tower's got more of a pattern to it," Prescott said. "Most human houses do, and I'm not just talking about big city skyscrapers. *Our* houses do. Same with log cabins — and even the thousand-year-old Anasazi cliff dwellings we learned about in social studies."

"Funny you should mention those Anasazi cliff dwellings," Mr. Flask said. "You'd agree that they're basically houses made of mud and stone, built into the side of a cliff?"

Prescott nodded.

Mr. Flask pulled a book from a shelf and thumbed through it. "Here are some cliff swallow nests. They're made of mud and built into the side of a cliff."

Alberta leaned over the book and laughed. "Cute! They look like lopsided balloons with short, fat periscopes on top. I guess the small openings help keep predators away from the babies."

The teacher nodded. "The nests' strong walls help, too. The adult cliff swallows construct them one clump of mud at a time, almost like a bricklayer with bricks."

Alberta looked up at Prescott. "Sounds like building a structure to me."

"The nests are round, while the Anasazi dwellings are square," Mr. Flask continued. "But as we learned, the square isn't the pinnacle of structural achievement."

Prescott studied the photo. "Those must be the weirdest nests in the world."

"Oh, I don't know." Mr. Flask turned the page. "The black tern builds a floating nest out of broken reeds." He flipped a few pages. "Weaver birds weave grasses into hanging nests." He turned one more page. "And here's one of my personal favorites. The edible-nest swiftlet builds its nest out of sticky strands of spit."

"What?" Luis left the habitats to look at the book. "Doesn't 'edible nest' mean —"

Mr. Flask nodded. "*Eatable nest.* Chefs in China use them to make a delicacy called bird's nest soup."

Suddenly, the door opened, and Dr. Kepler burst in. "We have a situation," she said to the teacher. "I think you'd better come with me."

Alberta perked up. "Maybe we could help?"

The principal frowned. "I doubt it, but you can come along if you want to."

Dr. Kepler led them out of the building and across the school yard to the bridge site. Long before they got there, they could tell what the "situation" was. Mrs. Hoof and her Daughters of Arcana were blocking the Parks Department crew's access to the building site. As they got closer, Prescott could make out some of the signs they were carrying. One read EINSTEIN ELEMENTARY EARNS AN F IN HISTORY. Another read WE SUPPORT TOWER POWER — SAVE THIS ARCANA LANDMARK! Off to one side sat Professor von Offel, grinning broadly.

"Hoo, boy," Luis muttered.

As they approached, Max darted out from behind a tree and ran up to the teacher. "Mr. Fla-ask!" he wailed. "I had nothing to do with this — I swear!"

"Don't worry, Max," the teacher said. "I don't know a single kid, or even a grown-up, who has control over his or her mother."

"Thanks," Max mumbled, and darted back behind the tree.

"Mrs. Hoof," Dr. Kepler began, "I've brought Mr. Flask here as you requested. Now, what can we do to address your concerns?"

"It's simple," Mrs. Hoof said. "Pledge some of that grant money to restore the von Offel tower."

"I take your concerns very seriously," the teacher said. "But I talked to an engineer friend, and she said that even if we used the entire grant, it still wouldn't be enough to restore that tower. In fact, it would be cheaper to put up a whole new tower."

"How is that possible?" Mrs. Hoof said scornfully. "I demand you get a new expert."

Mr. Flask shook his head. "Any expert would agree that the von Offel tower isn't structurally sound. For starters, it doesn't have any cross bracing."

"But that's part of its charm!" Mrs. Hoof objected. "And part of its historic importance."

The principal stepped in. "Cross bracing isn't decorative, Mrs. Hoof," she said. "It's an important structural feature."

Max's mother looked at Dr. Kepler skeptically.

"Mrs. Hoof, have you even *seen* the von Offel tower?" the principal continued.

Mrs. Hoof's eyebrows knit together for a moment. "My anonymous watchdog included a sketch —"

"I mean the actual tower, as it stands — barely stands, that is — today," Dr. Kepler said.

Mrs. Hoof shook her head. "I've been so busy with this campaign I haven't had the time," she admitted.

Mr. Flask gestured across the river. "You can see it this very afternoon, if the parks crew can get working on this bridge. Come back for sixth-grade science, and we'll take the first official field trip to the nature preserve. You can see both towers, and we can pick up this discussion at that point."

Mrs. Hoof looked back at her demonstrators. They took it as a sign to begin chanting "Don't Topple the Tower! Don't Topple the Tower!" The professor smiled and beat out the rhythm with one foot.

"The Daughters of Arcana has made its point," Dr. Kepler shouted over them. "You want important historical structures to be preserved. Now, I ask you to step aside and let the parks crew build the bridge."

Mrs. Hoof sighed. She swiped a finger across her neck, and the chanting stopped. Then she tucked her sign under her arm and started toward the parking lot, the rest of the Daughters of Arcana behind her. As she passed Max's hiding place behind the tree, her head tilted toward him. "Watch out for splinters, darling!" she called.

Max shuddered.

CHAPTER 7

Cross Bracing Is for Sissies

That afternoon, Mrs. Hoof met Mr. Flask's sixth graders in the science lab and followed them to the bridge site. The steel girders were in place, as were the planks across them. A rope was strung from one side of the river to the other, forming a temporary handrail.

The professor motioned toward the rope. "That rope is perfectly adequate as it is, Flask. Foregoing the wooden handrail will surely free up funds for the von Offel tower." He turned toward Mrs. Hoof. "As this charming lady has asked you to do."

Mrs. Hoof took a tentative step onto the bridge. She peered over the shaky rope and down to the water below. "I don't know, Professor," she said slowly. "There *will* be younger children crossing this bridge."

The professor grinned and waved her concerns away. "Challenges such as this build character," he said. "Sometimes I believe we coddle our youngsters too much."

"I suppose you could be right," Mrs. Hoof said, nervously searching the group for Max.

"After all," the professor continued, "do you think the children who work in our nation's coal mines get strong wooden guardrails?" He pounded his fist into his open palm. "Certainly not! They must fend for themselves. And it makes them tough as nails — at least the ones who avoid injury."

Mrs. Hoof gave the professor a funny look. "Children in coal mines? But you do remember that the United States outlawed child labor in the late 1930's?"

The professor's right eyebrow quivered. Atom laughed, then covered it with a series of short squawks.

"Naturally," the professor said. "Did I say no handrails? I meant no children. I apologize for my mistake. The brouhaha over our family tower has me a bit muddled."

Mrs. Hoof smiled sympathetically and patted the professor's arm. "I'm touched that you're so attached to your family history," she said. "It must be a magnificent tower."

Mr. Flask had politely stayed out of the discussion to this point, but now he stepped forward and got the class's attention. "Please line up single file to cross the bridge. I'll stand on the other end to steady the rope. Mrs. Hoof, could you steady the rope on this end?"

Max's mother nodded, though she looked reluctant to join the teacher in any undertaking.

The class crossed quietly and carefully, followed by Mrs. Hoof and the professor. Mr. Flask led them into the woods on a newly cut trail. After about five minutes, a tower came into view.

"It might be a little rusty in a few places," Mrs. Hoof said. "But it looks perfectly straight, strong, and sound to me."

"My engineer friend says the same thing," Mr. Flask said.

Mrs. Hoof clapped her hands. "Then we're in agreement. The von Offel tower will be preserved for future generations to enjoy!" She turned to the professor and smiled.

He did not smile back. "That," he said between gritted teeth, "is the Flask fire tower."

Mrs. Hoof's smile dissolved. "I see," she said.

Mr. Flask, meanwhile, was smiling broadly. "In less than two weeks, this fire tower should be open for classes to visit," he told his sixth graders.

"Excellent!" Sean shouted. "Remember that egg you dropped off the ladder when we were studying fragile space shuttle payloads? Let's try dropping one from the tower!"

Mr. Flask laughed. "We'll see, Sean. I certainly don't want you dropping anything from the tower without an adult present."

The professor cleared his throat loudly. "I believe

we're here to see the von Offel tower?" he said coldly.

The teacher nodded and gestured for the class to follow. In less than a minute, they reached a clearing. On the other side loomed a huge rust-covered column of deformed metal. Each beam was badly twisted, and some were even torn. More notably, the top of the tower was bent at an astonishing angle.

Mrs. Hoof looked stunned. "It's — it's — it's —" she began.

The professor smiled. "Don't worry, dear lady. You're not the first young woman struck speechless by von Offel genius. Perhaps you were going to say that it has all of the historic charm of the Leaning Tower of Pisa?"

Mrs. Hoof began trembling with anger. "I was going to say that it's a hazardous eyesore!" she said sharply.

The professor laughed. "Nothing a little spit and polish won't fix. Then the youngsters can climb up and do their science activities."

Mrs. Hoof exploded. "Are you crazy?" she screamed at the professor. "Are you actually suggesting I'd allow my baby to climb that monstrosity? Never!" She looked around the group, wild-eyed.

Max hid behind Sean, but not quickly enough.

"Max," his mother shouted. "You're coming with me! We're going to march straight to that principal's office and make certain that —" Her voice trailed off as she stormed away.

Mr. Flask glanced at the professor and was surprised to see that he actually looked disheartened. He thought for a moment. "Maybe you'd like to apply for a grant to stabilize the tower?" he asked finally. "I'd be happy to help you. Perhaps a little cross bracing —" He stopped, eyeing the vacant look on the older man's face. "Are you okay, Professor?"

"Cross bracing is for sissies," the professor mumbled. Then he turned on his heel and walked slowly back down the path.

Atom launched himself into the air and took a corkscrew path up around the von Offel tower. Then he dove back to ground level and started after the professor.

Mr. Flask looked up at the tower.

"What a hunk of junk!" Sean said.

The teacher ignored him.

Alberta raised her hand. When Mr. Flask didn't notice, she spoke up anyway. "Doesn't it look like it might fall over?"

The teacher sighed. "I was just thinking that in a sense it already has." He turned toward Alberta. "What I mean is, we just saw Professor von Offel's vision of his grand ancestral tower tumble to the earth."

Luis made a face. "Don't you think it should have? I mean, look at this bucket of bolts — or *rivets*, I guess."

Prescott reached down and dug something out of

the dirt. He held it up — a bowed and rusty metal cylinder. "Looks like it's already short one rivet." He searched the ground around him. "Maybe more."

Mr. Flask reached absently for the broken rivet. "I've just never seen the professor look that way."

His thoughts were interrupted by a familiar voice.

"Mr. Fla-a-sk!" Max came running up, panting heavily.

"Are you all right, Max?" Mr. Flask asked.

"Dr. Kepler said to find you," he gasped. "There's a big thunderstorm coming."

Off in the distance, they heard a low rumble.

Mr. Flask turned back down the path and motioned for the class to follow. "The closest safe shelter is the school building. The storm still sounds pretty far away, but we'd better move fast, just to be on the safe side."

CHAPTER 8

A Flash of Inspiration?

Not long after the sixth graders were safely back inside the lab, sheets of rain were coming down, and lightning was beginning to flash across the darkened sky.

Down the hall, in the professor's office, Atom looked back and forth between the window and his master. *BOOM!* The sound of thunder sent Atom a foot into the air.

The professor leaned back in his chair and sighed. "Perhaps it's just as well, how things turned out. If Flask leaves the von Offel tower alone, that means no pesky kids crawling all over it. I can have it all to myself, should I ever think of anything I need to use it for."

"Look on the bright side," Atom said. "You don't have to worry about the dangers of climbing that death trap. After all, you're already dead."

"I'm only 35 percent dead, remember?" the professor said, slumping into his chair.

"Hey, that's the first time I've heard you mention

that for days," Atom said. "Where's your latest plan for coming fully back to life?"

The professor shrugged.

Atom shook his feathered head. "I'm getting worried about you, Johannes. Where's your edge? Where's your fiery determination?" He watched the professor sink deeper and deeper into his chair.

Atom hopped to the window. A lightning bolt streaked across the sky. Less than a second later, thunder shook the building, and Atom was hit with his own bolt of inspiration. He turned toward the professor. "Johannes! Look out the window! It's your turn to catch another lightning bolt like the one that turned me into the World's Only Genius Parrot."

"That bolt was meant for me," the professor said darkly.

"That's right," the bird replied. "And birdbrained that I was, I stole it from you."

Flash. *BOOM!* Another bolt of lightning, followed by the roar of thunder.

The bird jabbed at the window with one wing. "Look, those lightning bolts are out there, just begging to be caught. I could fly home and dredge up the old cooking pot and wire. I could meet you in half an hour at —"

"The von Offel tower!" The professor's eyes flashed. He leaped to his feet. "Thank you for bringing me to my senses."

Atom gazed into the professor's eyes. "Just doing my duty."

The professor reached over him and pushed open the window. "Get going, you sluggish sack of giblets!"

Atom beamed. "Now that's the professor I know and love — know and respect — *know*." He took off into the storm.

Twenty minutes later, every desk in the science lab was crowned with a little house of cards. Alberta beamed at her three-story masterpiece. Prescott doggedly made his sixth try at a third story.

Luis was rearranging the cards in his first story and frowning. "There's got to be a way to work triangles into this. Maybe if I used tape?"

Prescott groaned as his building collapsed again. "Tape would help," he agreed. "But it would take away the challenge."

"No, it wouldn't," Alberta insisted. "It would just change the challenge, that's all." She raised her hand. "After we're done, Mr. Flask, could we see how high we can build if we use tape?"

Mr. Flask was staring at Professor von Offel's empty desk, a funny look on his face.

"Mr. Flask?" Alberta asked.

The teacher shook himself. "I'm sorry, Alberta. I was just thinking about Professor von Offel. I was hoping he'd join us for the rest of class. But he seems to be taking this stuff about the von Offel tower pretty personally. He really seems to identify with his great-great-great-great-great grandfather, Johannes von Offel."

"Mr. Fla-ask!" Max's hand swept through the air. "There's a good reason for that."

"Family pride!" Prescott shouted out.

Max glared at Prescott.

"Hey, isn't that Atom?" Heather pointed at the window.

Through the pouring rain, Prescott could make out the figure of a parrot flying toward the new bridge and pulling — a red wagon?

"Do you think he's headed for that rickety old metal tower?" Heather asked. "In the middle of a thunderstorm?"

Mr. Flask looked at Luis. "Could you run and see if the professor's in his office?"

Luis darted out the door. Ten seconds later he returned, shaking his head.

Mr. Flask bit his lower lip. "If Atom's going to the von Offel tower, you can bet that the professor's headed there as well." The teacher crossed to his closet and pulled out a yellow rain slicker and hat. "He could get hurt out there. I'm going to have to go after him."

BOOM! Thunder shook the classroom.

"You can't go out in a lightning storm," Prescott objected. "You've told us that more people are killed each year by lightning than by tornadoes and hurricanes combined."

"That's on average, of course," Alberta said.

Prescott shrugged. "My point is that it's incredibly dangerous."

Mr. Flask managed a smile. "Sounds like you guys really listened to my lightning safety rules. What else do you remember?"

Alberta raised her hand. "Well, as soon as you see lightning or hear thunder, head to a safe shelter, a real building like a house or school, not a garden shed."

"Ooh — that's a big mental stretch," Sean scoffed. "Especially since we all just did that. Please tell me you can do better than that."

"Come on, Sean," Mr. Flask said as he buttoned his raincoat. "Alberta was just giving the most vital facts first."

"Okay, answer me this," Sean said to Alberta. "Most cars are safe shelters, as long as you have the doors and windows closed. But what kind of car *isn't* safe?"

Alberta thought for a moment, then smiled. "A convertible," she said. "And even in a regular car, you have to be careful not to touch any metal. Now, here's a challenge question for you, Sean. Once you're inside a safe building, name five things you shouldn't do."

"That's more like *five* challenge questions for me,"

Sean grumbled. He counted off on his fingers. "Okay. Don't talk on a phone. Don't turn on the water in a sink or bathtub. Don't go near the windows or doors." He thought for a moment. "What else is there?"

Prescott frowned. "You're not supposed to touch anything electrical, so I guess you shouldn't wear a stereo headset."

"It's really not safe to touch *any* metal that's connected to the building or an electrical appliance, including plumbing pipes and cable wires," Luis added.

"I'll accept both of those," Alberta said. "But I'm thinking of one more safety rule that Sean would have a hard time following." She smiled at Sean's look of growing irritation. "Here's a hint: It has to do with a large metal appliance in the kitchen that's full of food."

"The fridge?" Sean asked. "I can't even touch the fridge? That's too harsh to be true."

Alberta crossed her arms triumphantly. "Believe it. I read about someone who got electrocuted during a lightning storm while she was holding the handle of her refrigerator."

The bell rang.

Mr. Flask finished tying his rain hat under his chin. "You forgot one of the most important rules," he said as the sixth graders gathered up their stuff. "Stay inside your safe shelter until at least a half hour after you see the last lightning or hear the last thunder. Well, I'll see you all tomorrow." He walked to the door.

"But you're not even following your own lightning safety rules!" Prescott said.

Mr. Flask nodded gravely. "Ordinarily, I wouldn't venture out into a storm like this. But I feel a responsibility toward Professor von Offel."

Sean made a face. "If the professor is a science expert, shouldn't he know the lightning rules? Isn't he responsible for his own safety?"

Mr. Flask sighed. "He *should* know the rules." He paused. "But you may have noticed that he seems a little — out of touch — sometimes. Besides, he's upset about his family tower, so he may not be thinking clearly. The bottom line is that his life is in danger."

"No, it isn't!" Max said. He turned to Prescott. "You're his lab assistant. Aren't you even going to tell him?"

Mr. Flask looked from Max to Prescott. "Tell me what? Do you have some reason to believe that the professor isn't out in the storm?"

Prescott looked down and shook his head.

Max threw up his hands. "The professor's life isn't in danger, because he's not alive!" he said. "Professor John von Offel is the ghost of Johannes von Offel!"

Mr. Flask rolled his eyes. "Not you, too," he said, and walked out the door.

Prescott grabbed Luis and Alberta. "We've got to do something to stop him. Max is right. Mr. Flask is risking his life for nothing!"

Luis nodded. "At this point, so what if the professor is exposed and Mr. Flask loses his chance at the Vanguard Teacher Award?"

"Maybe he'll believe us if we tell him about Prescott's videotape," Alberta said. She ran out into the hallway with Luis and Prescott close behind. "Wait, Mr. Flask!" she shouted. "We have something important to tell you!"

The teacher waited for them to catch up. "Okay, but make it quick. The storm is getting worse by the minute."

Alberta nudged Luis.

"Um, Max's ghost story may *sound* crazy," Luis began, "but we know that it's true."

"Guys, I don't have time for this," Mr. Flask said. "We've been over this more than once." He turned to leave.

Alberta grabbed the sleeve of his raincoat. "But this time we have proof," she said. "It's a videotape that absolutely, positively shows that the professor is a ghost. We can bring it to you this afternoon if you'll just agree to stay inside."

Mr. Flask gently removed Alberta's fingers from his sleeve. "Look, I know you're all concerned about my safety. And it's clear that you think you have something important on video. I'll tell you what. I'd be happy to look at your tape some other time. But for now, I really have to trust my instincts." He took the last few steps to the door, gave them a quick smile and wave, then disappeared into the storm.

CHAPTER 9

"Hey, My Fist Didn't Go Through Him!"

B y this time the professor had scrambled up as high as he could on the crooked von Offel tower.

"I'd forgotten how exhilarating this is," he yelled down to Atom.

The parrot was struggling to drag a large iron cooking pot up the swaying steps. "I'd forgotten how terrifying, dangerous, and foolhardy it is," Atom replied.

BOOM! The thunder sent Atom into the air again. "You know, Johannes," he shouted, "the more I think about it, the more I realize that it couldn't have been the electricity that made me smart. More likely, my intelligence comes from superior genes."

"Not a chance!" the professor roared over the storm. "Your mother was just as birdbrained as you were before your lucky brush with electricity."

Atom sniffed loudly as he heaved the iron pot onto the platform. "You didn't have to drag my mother into this," he muttered.

The professor pulled a piece of wire out of his

pocket. He wound one end around the pot handle and the other end around the tower's metal frame. Then he lowered the pot onto his head like an oversized beanie. "Enlighten me!" he yelled into the storm. He tipped up one edge of the pot and caught Atom's eye. "Get it?" he grinned. "En-*light*-en —"

BOOM! "This is getting on my nerves," Atom shouted up at the professor. "I'm going to look for someplace safer." He hopped up on the railing and surveyed the treetops below. "Since we're standing at the top of the tallest structure around, which also happens to be metal, just about anyplace would qualify as safer."

"Are you a parrot or a chicken?" the professor shouted.

Atom shrugged and flew off into the rain.

Professor von Offel watched Atom descend toward the treetops with disdain. Then something yellow caught his eye.

"It can't be," he told himself. He shouted into the rain, "Atom! Get your tail feathers up here!"

The parrot was already landing on the railing behind him. "It's Flask!" he reported. "He's calling for you to come down." Atom peered down over the railing. "Uh-oh, it looks like he's going to climb up. I thought he was smarter than that."

"He's after my extra brainpower!" the professor shouted.

"I doubt it," Atom replied. "It's more likely that he's trying to save your life."

The professor made a face. "That *would* be like a meddling Flask. Either way, I want you to stop him!"

Atom jumped off the guardrail and spiraled down to the base of the tower. Mr. Flask was standing at the bottom step, looking up uneasily. Atom took another lap around the tower to build up speed, then pointed his beak straight at the teacher.

Mr. Flask noticed him just in time to vault out of the way. "Shoo, Atom!" he shouted.

The parrot made a tight turn and dive-bombed the teacher again. Then he made another turn and another attack. He kept up a full-scale assault. When he had driven Mr. Flask dozens of yards away, he stopped and perched in a tree.

Mr. Flask eyed Atom warily. Then he looked up at the professor, who was gripping the metal guardrail of the swaying tower. The teacher gritted his teeth. "This is a matter of life and death," he told himself. "I can't let a little bird stop me." He took a step toward the tower.

Atom launched himself off his tree branch and drove Mr. Flask back an additional five yards.

"Okay," Mr. Flask muttered. "There's more than one way to skin a parrot." He unbuttoned his raincoat and waved it like a bright yellow flag, hoping to get the professor's attention.

BOOM! Atom fluttered up and banged his head on the branch above.

Mr. Flask looked around. "Those are definitely getting closer. I've got to make a run for von Offel."

BOOM! A lightning bolt flashed overhead and struck the top of the tower. It blasted the professor, knocking him into the guardrail. The top of the tower lurched sideways with a loud creak. It bounced a few times like a sprung jack-in-the-box. Finally, a rivet snapped, then another, then another, until the whole tower toppled to the ground.

Atom quickly searched the wreckage for the professor and landed on his chest. "Are you okay, Johannes? And do you feel any smarter?"

The professor's eye rolled back in its socket. "Is that you, Mother dear?"

A few feet away, Mr. Flask lay trapped by a fallen metal beam. I must be in worse shape than I feel, he thought. It sounded like that parrot was talking in sentences. He struggled for a few seconds to move the fallen beam, but it wouldn't budge. Finally, he leaned his head back and passed out.

When Mr. Flask finally came to, he was staring up into Dr. Kepler's concerned face.

"We've called the paramedics," she said. "Help is on its way." She tucked a blanket around him.

"I'm okay," he told her. "Just trapped." He noticed the lab assistants behind her. "I thought I told you guys to stay inside."

"We did," Alberta told him quietly. "I guess you must have been out for a while." She looked over at the professor, who was stumbling around in circles. "I suppose he wasn't in any shape to go for help."

Max ran over to the teacher. "Look, Mr. Flask! The professor isn't leaving any footprints!"

The teacher suppressed a groan. "This really isn't a great time, Max."

The professor swerved and started a wide circle around the group.

"Hey, wait," Prescott said. "Actually, he is leaving footprints!" He shared a look with Alberta and Luis.

Dr. Kepler watched them with suspicion. "Why shouldn't the professor leave footprints?" she asked.

"Explain this, then," Max said, striding up to the dazed professor. "Why can I do this?" He shot out his fist and punched von Offel in the gut. The professor doubled over.

"Max!" The principal ran to von Offel's side.

Max looked down at his hand. "Hey, my fist didn't go through him!"

Dr. Kepler helped the stunned professor sit down on the ground. "That surprises you, Max? You were supposed to master the properties of solids in third grade."

Max ran over to Heather. "Give me your mirror."

"Why would I carry a mirror?" Heather objected.

Max threw up his hands. "There's not a single sixth-grade boy who doesn't watch every move you make," he said. "You think none of us noticed that you carry a mirror in your left rear pocket?"

"Oh, all right," Heather said. She pulled out a compact and passed it to Max.

Max ran back to the principal and thrust the compact at her. "Look for the professor's reflection in this mirror. I guarantee you won't find it. I'll stake my B+ average on it."

"This is ridiculous!" the principal said. "The professor is a guest in our school, and —"

Dr. Kepler looked around at the scene. Could it really be more absurd than anything else that had happened here? She opened the compact and tilted it toward the professor. "You're wrong, Max. I see him very clearly."

Max snatched the compact and looked for himself. "But how?"

Atom swooped down from a tree branch and grabbed the mirror in his talons. He flew over the professor and dropped it into his outstretched hand.

The professor peered into the mirror. "I'm alive!" he shouted. "I'm 100 percent alive!"

Dr. Kepler turned to Max. "After this is all over, I'd like to have a little talk with you."

"But something must have happened during that thunderstorm," Max whined. "Before that, he was a ghost! He practically admitted it! Didn't you just hear him sound surprised that he's alive?"

The principal looked around at the tangled remains of the von Offel tower. "If I'd been hit by lightning and fallen from that height, I'd be *flabbergasted* that I was alive."

Later that afternoon, the lab assistants met Mr. Flask outside the hospital. He was limping but had no serious injuries.

"I was incredibly lucky," he told them. "More amazingly, the professor walked away an hour ago with a completely clean bill of health."

"They didn't find *anything* unusual about him?" Prescott asked.

"Not a thing," the teacher said. "Hey, Prescott. My memory's a little fuzzy because of the pain, but wasn't there a videotape you wanted me to see?"

Prescott looked at Alberta and Luis. They shrugged.

"I think it turns out to be obsolete data," Luis said.

Over at the von Offel mansion, the professor angrily kicked a blanket off his legs. "Without an afghan, it's too cold. With an afghan, it's too hot. This is no way to live!"

"The key word is *live*," Atom said. "You've been trying to become fully alive for months. Didn't you ever stop to think about what that would mean? In case you've forgotten, living people get cold, hot, sleepy, sore, hungry —"

"Ah, that's what that pain in my abdomen is!" the professor exclaimed. "It's been so long, I hardly recognized it. During my partially corporeal existence, I only ate and drank as an amusing experiment. But I remember now — this rumbling means I'm hungry!" He looked around. "What do we have to eat?"

Atom raised a feathered eyebrow. "Bird seed — nothing but bird seed. I believe I've said a word or two on this matter. Maybe now that *you* have to eat, we'll get a little decent chow around here."

The professor sniffed indignantly. "Bird seed is a perfectly respectable food."

Atom waved a claw toward his food dish. "Then please help yourself."

"Indeed I will." The professor scooped out a handful of seeds and poured them into his mouth. He chewed them experimentally. "Firm and crunchy, with a faint essence of barnyard," he pronounced. He reached for another handful. "I can't believe you've been hoarding this delicacy for yourself!"

Atom watched with disbelief as the professor emptied his food dish. "That's the last of my bird seed," the parrot told him. "Maybe you'd like to try something different?"

The professor stood up and slipped on his coat. "An excellent plan, Atom. There was something at the grocery store that caught my eye last time."

Atom perched excitedly on his shoulder. "Let me guess, crab cakes? No, no — porterhouse steak?"

The professor shook his head. "It was a specialty blend called Oats 'n Groats."

"Wait a minute," Atom said. "That sounds suspiciously like —"

The professor nodded cheerfully. "Bird seed!"

Welcome to the World of
MAD SCIENCE!

The Mad Science Group has been providing live, interactive, exciting science experiences for children throughout the world for more than 12 years. Our goal is to provide children with fun, entertaining, and exciting activities that instill a clearer understanding of what science is really about and how it affects the world around them. Founded in Montreal, Canada, we currently have 125 locations throughout the world.

Our commitment to science education is demonstrated throughout this imaginative series that mixes hilarious fiction with factual information to show how science plays an important role in our daily lives. To add to the learning fun, we've also created exciting, accessible experiment logs so that children can bring the excitement of hands-on science right into their homes.

To discover more about Mad Science and how to bring our interactive science experience to your home or school, check out our website:
http://www.madscience.org

We spark the imagination and curiosity of children everywhere!